Graven Imag...

Graven Image

Charlie Williams

CRIME EXPRESS

Graven Image
by Charlie Williams

Published in 2011 by Crime Express
Crime Express is an imprint of
Five Leaves Publications,
PO Box 8786, Nottingham NG1 9AW
www.fiveleaves.co.uk

ISBN: 978 1 907869 10 5

© Charlie Williams, 2011

Crime Express 10

Five Leaves acknowledges financial support
from Arts Council England

Five Leaves is represented by Turnaround
and distributed by Central Books.

Cover design: Gavin Morris

Typeset and design;
Four Sheets Design and Print

Printed by Imprint Digital in Great Britain

1.

I was in the abbey when I realised I'd have to burn for my sins.

If you go round the cloisters and have a look at all the stained glass windows, you'll find one of a man being burned to death, and he looks a bit like me, if I was white and had a beard. And even if he didn't look like me, I straight away knew all about him. I didn't know who he was or what he'd done, but I knew he was paying for something he'd done, and that he'd had no choice but to do that thing. I could see myself going the same way. And soon.

Saying that, I hoped I was wrong.

Getting burned to death seemed a bit harsh.

I turned, spotting someone come round the corner. I knew this was no abbey-going punter. No punter moves with that kind of purpose, eyes burning a hole in your skull from fifty yards. The cloisters are four big corridors surrounding a nice garden that you can look at through the windows but not go in, and I was stood halfway along one side. Behind me was the gift shop and the main part of the abbey. Habit had me making a mental note of that in case things turned serious and I needed a way out. But I knew I wouldn't be needing that mental note. I had hope, didn't I? Things could be sorted.

Burnings could be avoided.

"Where's Graven?" I said to the oncoming ned with his chin up, arms swinging a foot adrift of his hips, bigging himself up big-time. He was all of five foot five and built like a variety-sized box of cornflakes. Twenty yards shy and he reaches inside his hoodie. Not a good sign.

Things weren't just turning serious, they were starting out that way.

House of God and all.

He was five paces away now and I could make out his eyes, but they weren't on me like those of a good blade boy should be. Or even a shit one, really. It was around then I came to wonder if I might be wrong, if this one here was nothing to do with Graven's dirty workings. Could be he was Mr Average, headed for the gift shop, after a nice key-ring or an embossed prayer book. Especially with his hand still in his top and not producing the stainless. Mind you, does Mr

Average keep his hood up inside the house of God? I don't know, but I had mine up.

I had good reason to.

He pulled alongside, the hand coming out now. This is where it got a bit odd for me. Meaning unusual things started going on up there in my head. I mean, your first instinct is self-preservation, right? Someone's about to flash a tool, you either show him your heels or toss him a pre-emptive set of knuckles. This had been my way for as long as I could remember.

But I got a different thing occurring to me this time. It occurred to me — with the sun bursting out behind my head, flashing the colours of that burning man across the ned's grey Diesel with a big black 50 across the front — that I could always just take it. I could let him do what he'd been sent to do.

Why prolong the inevitable? I mean, what the fuck is life, really and truly?

One long trail of shit stretching day to day.

Until you die.

That's why I closed my eyes. Serious, that is the reason. Bring it on, I was thinking, send me to the big fucking sleep from which no cunt awakes. And when I opened them again I saw an angel approaching, coming down a long tunnel. Or maybe it was a leery-eyed vicar walking down the cloisters in my direction, I realised after blinking a few times. I now had a letter under my arm. A sealed envelope, brown smudges all over one corner and some damp on another. I sniffed it.

Soil.

The ned was nowhere. Common sense said he was in the main abbey, hiking sharpish for the exit after doing his drop-off. Which meant he was actually in the gift shop, because I knew how his sort operated and it wasn't via common sense. I went in there, stuffing the letter down my arse pocket where it belonged. He was browsing your more expensive class of gift down the far aisle, where the old dear at the counter couldn't clock him. I yanked his hood down and swung him back, sending him crashing into a rotating postcard stand. Then I dragged him to the door, all eight stone of him. I was sorry about trashing the shop but there were more pressing matters just now. Before I could get him out he wriggled free of the Diesel and scuttled behind the counter.

The old dear was backed up to the wall, hand on heart.

I apologised to her and grabbed the ned by the ankle, intending to get him away and thereby give her heart a rest. She didn't seem to appreciate my efforts there, looking at her, but that's not what it's about, is it? It's about respecting boundaries. It's about making sure your bad shit doesn't fuck up innocent people.

"The fuck's this?" I said to the ned. I was kneeling on his back. His T-shirt was riding up and you could see part of a large koi carp tat on his ribs, outlined and long healed but never coloured in.

"What?"

"This!" I was still trying to get the letter out of my pocket.

"What?"

"Shut the fuck up a minute!"

I finally got it out and shoved it in his face.

"This!"

"I don't fuckin' know! I'm just —"

"Don't you swear in a lady's presence, you little —"

"You're hurtin' me!"

I probably was, to be fair. I'm no goliath but I do like a pie. And I can handle myself. I got off him. None of this was turning out like I'd hoped. Straight away he bolted for the door. I didn't bother going after him. I was knackered, inside and out.

"I'll tell you what you are!" the ned was shouting from the glass doorway, spit flying. "You're a fuckin' spanner!"

I shrugged at the old dear and started picking up the rotating postcard display.

2.

QUITS.

That's what it said on a piece of paper inside that soil-stained envelope, in big block capitals. I'm no expert but I thought it might have been written by a female. There was a careful curve to the letters that you saw in Kelly's handwriting, although Kelly wrote with a bit more confidence than seen here. That's all you can give a kid, if you ask me. Confidence. And a surname.

And a big hug every day.

"Quits?" I said.

I was walking through town, keeping to back streets. I'd long since read the letter, such as it was, but it was still messing with my head and making no sense. How could we be quits? I'd been waiting for a blade in the guts, back there at the abbey — that's how far in Graven's debt

I was. And we're not talking loans here. I'm on about the currency of grievance, where eyes and teeth are exchanged in violent transactions.

See, I'd fucked up. About a week ago, this was, during which time I'd been hiding out in the sticks. I'd still be there now if I hadn't got that text from Graven. Let's get this sorted, he'd suggested. Life's too short for grudges and contracts on the heads of former friends and loyal compadres, so let's meet up, shout at each other a bit and then have a little hug.

If he thought I was hugging him he could kiss my black arse. And if I thought he wanted to make up, my black arse deserved the kicking it had coming.

So why had I come back? Homesickness? Had exile got me down... all that country air making me hanker for the polluted streets I knew? Bollocks had it.

I missed my daughter.

And that is the only reason.

What it was, just so you know, is that I'd gone overboard with my duties and someone had got hurt. Very hurt, if blood and exposed bone is anything to go by. Which wouldn't be a problem on any normal day — people were always getting a bit hurt where my job was concerned, sometimes in life-changing ways. But they're not normally Graven's VIP guest.

Even if he did have it coming.

So you can see why I was expecting some sort of violent retribution, that being Graven's preferred method of disciplinary procedure. And you can see why I was scratching my head over this 'QUITS' business.

How had the score been evened? The inconvenience of having to go to the abbey at 4pm, standing Kelly up and missing one of our precious rendezvous? The indignity of having to joust with that ned in the gift shop? Was it all about that dirty envelope? What does anthrax look like? Maybe I was a goner already, just by touching the paper. What was that film where they did that?

I got my phone out and rang Darren. I needed him in the game with me. Graven and his crew were the only ones who knew I was back in town and I didn't like it that way. You need an ally in your corner, someone to notice when you go missing. Plus I wanted to run this 'QUITS' bollocks past him. Darren could always see the angles where I had a blind-spot.

But he wasn't answering just now.

I went to pocket the phone but it went off in my hand. I answered, thinking it was Darren on the ring-back. I should have looked who the caller was. I could have prepared myself.

"Darren?" I said, trying to light a fag with my

spare hand. "Look, I got a bit of a situ —"

"Where is she?"

"What? Who's —?"

"Who d'you think it is? It's Jane, OK? Where is she?"

Jane being my ex, of course. I dropped my unlit fag.

"Where's Kelly?" she shouted.

"I dunno! How should I know? Injunction says I can't come within fifty metres of her, remember?"

"Oh shut up! I know you see her! You think I'm stupid? You think I dunno you meet in that nasty pub on Wednesdays after school?"

"Thursdays."

"What? Oh yeah, that's what I meant."

"And it's not a nasty pub, that's the whole point."

"What are *you* doing going there, then?"

"What's that supposed to —?"

"Where is she?"

"Look, I never met her today. I had to —"

"You know where she is or not?"

"No! I swear I —"

"Don't bother swearing. If you want to help, just go and look for Kerry."

"Alright, but she's... It's Kelly, by the way."

"That's what I said."

"Was it? Oh... Look, she's probably gone to her

friend's house or something."

"Whatever. And you owe me some mon —"

I hung up. I'd heard all I needed to hear.

I remembered that film now:

The Name of the Rose.

3.

I expect you'll be wondering who the hell I am.

Leon was what they knew me as at school. My mum hated my dad so she wouldn't let me use his surname. She hated her dad as well so I couldn't use hers either. So I ended up just having LEON on all my name tags, written in marker because she couldn't sew. And she must have put that down on the forms and stuff when I started going there, because all the teachers called me Leon as well, even the ones who called you by your last name. You'd think a parent wouldn't get away with that. But then you didn't know my mum.

I used to hate having only one name. It made me the odd one out, even more than my colour did. It put me at a disadvantage compared to everyone else, with their surnames and middle names. I missed the middle name most. A middle name is like a secret identity you can use whenever you want. Or you can ditch the first name if you don't like it and just use the middle one. That's what my ex did, the mother of my only daughter. But she was advertising a weakness there, showing the world how they could get under her skin and hurt her.

Took me a long time but eventually I got used to having just one name. I felt like Pelé, or Eusébio. Except I wasn't as good as them at footy. I looked a bit like them as well, especially Eusébio. Maybe that was why people didn't make such a fuss about me having one name. They'd never have tolerated it if I was a white kid, but a little black boy... that's alright. "It's part of their culture," they'd say. "They do things different over there."

I never did find out where 'over there' was, but I found out I had a surname. All you have to do is look at your birth certificate. Sounds easy now, but it took until I was eighteen and mum was dead before I realised I even had such a thing. She'd kept it stashed under her bed, in a flat box with other bits and bobs. It's strange, the little objects a woman cares about.

Finally I had a surname, even if I didn't really want it any more. But I'd be getting married within a couple of years and my wife wanted to get rid of hers, so at least I had one to give her. And to Kelly, the daughter who'd be coming along after that.

Anyway, so Leon is who I am name-wise.

Job-wise, I wasn't so proud. Not everyone can be proud of how they earn a crust but we've all got to earn one somehow. And who says you've got to be proud of your job anyway? Being proud of your job is nothing to be proud of, if you ask me. So yeah, I was a brothel bouncer. I lent a certain presence to the foyer of Destiny Gentlemen's Club, up on the Makin Estate. Punters saw me when I came in and knew what they'd have to tangle with, should they choose to get lairy. And it worked, most times.

Punters come for sex, not aggro.

They want aggro, they can get it in any pub or club. They can't get sex there, though. Not the kind of punter you got in Destiny on a normal night. We are talking the calibre of man that prostitution was invented for. If they don't pay for it they don't get none of it at all. Or *you* get rapists. So, in a way, I was performing a public service.

Maybe I should be proud of my job after all.

When you looked at it, it really was a proper profession. You had specific skills learned from arduous training and on-the-job experience, and you were responsible for the welfare of others. So, yeah, I was a brothel bouncer. AKA Discreet Services Security Provider.

You're smirking, I see.

Think of it this way: who's there to keep order when a pub-load of pissed-up knob-ends walks up? Who steps in when there's a dispute over services rendered against monies due? Who's there with the arm-lock when a punter turns slap-happy?

I'll tell you something, a working girl cannot do it. Men are just stronger than women, end of. Especially when they're ten pints of wife-beater to the bad. Five women all pile on a strident punter, they're still not going to stop him doing what he wants.

See what I mean about responsibilities?

You can understand how you start seeing the girls as your family after a while, and punters as threats to your own flesh and blood. And when they hurt your family — *really* hurt her — there's only one kind of response.

I'll be telling you more about that.

Mind you, some women have ways of getting around a berserker. Some women can talk a person round just by looking at them in a certain way. Male or female, they're all butter to her hot knife. I'm talking about Carla.

We'll get to her as well.

4.

The Rose and Crown had a swinging sign out front that resembled neither rose nor crown. What it looked like was a big monster running towards you, listing to one side slightly like someone had speared it a while back and it had tried to carry on as normal, but blood loss was catching up and it was about to keel over. None of the other regulars could see it, even though I'd pointed it out to them. This was yet another area where I seemed to be out of step with the herd. What they saw was a very old and peeling painting of a crown with a rose in front of it. But I still got along alright with most of them. We had an understanding. They knew what I was about and didn't seem to judge me for it.

Which is why I didn't fuck about, going straight up to Jim, the landlord, and saying: "Kelly been in here?"

He glanced up from his paper and gave me a startled look. That's how intense I must have been coming across. "Kelly who?"

"Kelly, my... you know, the girl I bring in here Thursdays."

"Don't know her."

"What? Look, Jim, we sit on that table over —"

"Leon, you don't have to shout at me. I don't want any kind of trouble or disturbance in here. Get me?"

"Are you listening? All I'm asking is —"

"And all I'm asking is for you to keep your trouble away from this pub. We've welcomed you here, while other places perhaps wouldn't. Me and Madge don't like to judge, and we expect some respect in return. Get me?"

"Alright," I said, containing myself. "What happened?"

"This ain't that sort of pub, Leon. I'm sorry but I'd be happy if you stopped drinking here for a while."

"I'm just looking for my daughter, Jim! Have you seen her or not? About so high, slim, long curly hair, skin a bit lighter than mine..."

"I've seen nothing."

"For fuck's sake, Jim!"

Jim's son Jonathan stepped up to the bar beside me. He was hardly ever here and I knew something must have happened. He was a big lad, but soft, not having the upbringing like I'd had.

"You gotta leave our dad alone," he said, a tremor in his voice.

"Or else?"

"Or else whatever you want." Not so much of a tremor now. When something don't hurt them straight away, people get cocky fast. "You ain't getting any kind of answer here though, right? You got problems, mate, and you need to get 'em sorted. That's what I say."

I stepped away and sat for a moment at a table, getting my thoughts together. I knew I was being fucked around here but the question was why? From what I could see it was either:

1. Because they'd heard I was in the shit with Graven
2. That old dear in the gift shop was Jim's mum
3.
4. Because I'm black

Number four you've always got to consider from the day you're born until the day you die. Especially in a town like this. Even when people are being alright to you, you never know what's going on behind their pasty foreheads.

Numbers one and two, they could go fuck themselves if those were true.

Three I didn't even want to think about, let alone say out loud.

I couldn't.

If you say the words, they might come true.

I looked around the pub instead, recognising three or four of the ten or so in there, all of them acting like I didn't even exist. Cunts. I should have known I was only here on sufferance.

No, they weren't cunts really.

You couldn't blame them.

I'd have expected more to be in at this time though. Half six and no one was at the fruit machine. Early evening, Tyrone was normally on it, pissing away whatever he hadn't lost down the bookies at lunchtime.

I was wasting my time here. I knew I should admit that and go look elsewhere, but something kept me on my stool... something small and pink and shaped like a pyramid, I realised when I finally spotted it a couple of tables away. I only knew one person who could fold an empty crisp bag that way, and she did it with her prawn cocktail flavour every Thursday when I met her in here.

I went straight out the main door, not even looking back at the non-cunts who you couldn't really blame. As I went round the side I started getting a sick feeling in my guts, like someone was playing a bass guitar in there. I wanted to shit and puke at the same time, shout and punch walls because I knew what was happening here and I was powerless to fix it just now.

The toilets at the Rose and Crown are outdoor ones. You reach them from the back door but I didn't want the non-cunts to know I was there, so I went round the side. There were two cubicles in the bogs and one was closed and locked. I climbed on the wash basin and leaned over the partition, looking down at Tyrone, him of the fruit machine. He was picking his nose.

"I got shit on you," I said.

He jumped and made a little noise, then his nose started bleeding. I think he'd rammed his finger too far up it. "Look what you done!" he said, looking at me. "What did you do that for? You made me... erm..."

"You got two chances to give me the right answer. Fail once, you get the small forfeit. Fail twice, the big one. Get past 'em both and you're a winner."

"I dunno nothin' about no —!"

"Who'd she leave with?"

I didn't know for sure that she'd left with anyone, of course. She could have waited ages and then split, gone down her pal's house and no harm done. But she might not have.

"Who?"

"You know who."

"I don't! I —"

"My Kelly!"

"Your Kelly? Who the fuck's...? Oh."

"Yeah. Oh. Who'd she leave with?"

"Honest, I dunno, Leon."

I reached down and grabbed him by the hair. It was a bit short and well greasy, but I got enough of a grip and slammed his face against the door, saying: "There's your small forfeit."

I don't think he heard that over his own screaming.

I grabbed his hair again and he shut up.

"Second chance: who'd she leave with?"

He gave me his doe eyes. Actually they were more like a frog than a doe. A frog with blood all over his chin.

"What's the big forfeit?"

"Like I said, I got shit on you."

"What shit?"

"I work at Destiny, Ty. I see everyone come and go."

"Eh?"

I was on sabbatical, it's true. But you would be too if you'd maimed a VIP punter. Didn't mean I wouldn't be back there when this all blew over. Business is business.

"Don't play the thick one with me, Ty. You

want me to tell your mum what you like to do?"

"You stay away from my mam!"

He folded his arms and looked away in a sulk, breathing hard through his mouth. I could crack him in ten seconds. You watch.

"I can draw a diagram. Cindy told me all about it. By the way, she went in last week and had the full operation. Know what that makes her, Ty? 100% woman... sort of. I suppose you won't be so interested in her now, eh?"

"Fuck off, you nutter!"

Maybe just over, eleven seconds — fair play. I reached down and wiped a drip of blood off his chin, then wiped it on the white door amongst the footy teams and pictures of cocks and who shagged who.

"Who'd Kelly leave with?"

He looked at where I'd scrawled his blood, his breathing slowing as he said, almost so you couldn't hear:

"Carla?"

5.

LEVEL 1: BREACH IN PROTOCOL

1. *Record breach in security log inc. date, time and security personnel on shift*
2. *Appropriate tools obtained from security cabinet*
3. *Lock cabinet again after tools obtained*
4. *Investigate breach without delay*
5. *If no danger found, personnel responsible for false alarm to be reprimanded/penalised*
6. *If danger found, escalate alert to appropriate level*

Best if I just say what happened back there at Destiny, with the VIP and shit.

This was a couple of weeks ago. I'd popped out for some fags, over at the garage. Dennis Tamar was behind the counter and we chatted about footy for a while. Dennis had Everton down for relegation but I said not a chance, not unless Rooney got injured. I picked up a couple of other things while I was there too, fireworks and stuff. It was bonfire night, and I knew Kelly's mum wouldn't be doing anything to mark the occasion, being obsessed with health and safety. That kid would be a wet lettuce if it was just her mum, I swear. But she had me too, and no way was I going to let her grow up soft. One way or another, I'd make sure she had a proper bonfire, sparklers and everything.

I'm not really supposed to leave the premises. There's no saying what might happen and who might come in while I'm gone, but this was quite early — about three in the afternoon — and I'd never known a lairy punter at that time. Lairy is a by-product of alcohol, and the only drinkers that time of day are your committed ones, who are more interested in drink than sex. So I wasn't surprised when I got back and found the place all quiet.

Not even Carla was in her office. I checked the computer — only one girl was in just now, that new one. She was up in Room One, but I couldn't see if she had a punter there or not. I shook my head: this constituted a Level One breach of protocol. The amount of time I'd spent getting this security system set up and they don't even use it right. All they have to do is type their number into a keypad when they go in the room, then flick the switch to green or red depending on the punter situation, thereby letting muggins downstairs know who's where and what they're up to. How hard is that? But still they fucked it up. I could see a couple more training seminars being in order. They'd moan, sure. They'd whinge and whine and call me Gareth out of *The Office*. But they'd soon stop that if a punter went violent on them, oh yes. They'd be reaching for that red button and thanking the god of prostitution that their security man had gone to all that trouble for them.

I sat down at the computer, running through the Level One procedure in my head.

6.

Took me all of thirty minutes to get Carla's address. I thought that was quite good, bearing in mind this is a woman I do not get along with and only ever see in a purely business capacity. To give you the full picture, I fucking hated her. Something about her just got on my wick and stayed there, pinching and biting it. Listening to her was like poking darts in your ears, and looking at her was like scratching your eyeballs with that nail-file she was always using.

To be fair, I did understand the point of her. You need someone like that running a brothel. Just like you need someone like me handling security. As much as I hate to say it, we were a good management team.

I don't know why I was shocked, finding the place and seeing what a dump it was. True enough: she was a brothel madam, and you picture them living in tacky mini-mansions with pink curtains and a fountain in the front garden. But Graven was the owner of Destiny, not her. He paid her a wage, just like me. And it wasn't like she could just fuck off and find a better paid position. Besides a couple of Chinese ones that kept moving camp before you could hit them, Destiny was the only knocking shop in town.

She could like her salary or lump it.

And let's be clear, here: Graven don't take kindly to being lumped.

Which explained the crumbling town-house on Green Hill, chest-high weeds out front and five rusty doorbells beside the front door. I pressed number three, which I'd been told was Carla's.

Then I leaned on it.

Fuck, what was I doing? The way I guessed it, Carla had taken Kelly off and handed her over to Graven, who was holding her some-where, planning on using her as bait to force me to do some horrible thing in penance for my fuck-up. Which I'd gladly do, if it got Kelly free. There was no way Carla herself would be holding her. Carla was no different to Graven's men, doing what the fuck he says or else. But she still wouldn't want to face me right now. Glancing out her window and seeing me come along the road, she'd be out the back and down the fire escape in a shot.

I went round the back.

In a shot.

No way had she come down this thing in a hurry. Not without half the neighbourhood knowing about it anyway. I'm no expert on fire escapes but even I knew scrap iron when I saw it. Two or three tons of the stuff in what looked to be two thousand moving parts. What wasn't rusted to fuck was loose and rattling like a bag of change. There'd have to be some serious fucking blaze going on for any sane person to set foot on this heap of nails, let me tell you.

I set foot on it.

The doors on these old lodging houses are shit. I'm no housebreaker and even I had it open with no more fuss than a little scattering of white paint flakes on the floor. You didn't get a number round the back but I knew straight away it was Carla's. I could smell her. When you work in a house full of hookers, you learn about perfume, mouthwash and all kinds of fragranced detergents. I don't know what scent Carla used, but it fucking reeked.

No one in.

For one so organised in her working life, I'd never have guessed she was a such a slob at home. Bed unmade, clothes on the floor, empty wine bottles all around, bins overflowing and no sign of a Hoover. This wasn't just turning a blind eye to filth and disarray, we are talking a concerted effort to achieve it. It was like she was making up for the po-faced order of her job by having chaos at home. I hoped it was working out for her. I knew it was good for what I had in mind. A domestic setup as relaxed as this means a good chance you'll find some evidence. You can always do with evidence.

I mean, you can't take anyone's word for anything.

I started rooting around, grimacing as I slid a plate of half-eaten chow mein off a pile of papers. Most were bills, the rest made up of sun-bed sessions offered at two for one (a month free if you renew your health club membership NOW), a letter from the NHS asking her to come for a smear (dated eight months ago) and various final demands. A letter from a solicitor looked like it was to do with divorce proceedings, but I ignored it. I'd never been able to understand legal stuff and I had no hope now. And besides, it was fuck all to do with abducting a girl on behalf of a vindictive crime boss. So I looked elsewhere.

I was starting to give up hope of finding anything more interesting than a smiley face mug with five week's worth of penicillin growth in it when I found the box, under the bed, obscured by a black nightie with what looked like spunk stains on it. It was only a shoe box but you could see it was special. The sides were repaired with yellowed Sellotape and endless flowers had been doodled on the top in blue biro.

I knew the sort of thing I'd find inside, and I wasn't wrong: old letters, photographs, sentimental knick-knacks. I struggled to imagine Carla with a sentimental bone in her body, but there you go. One snap was of a younger Carla in a wedding dress, smiling and looking like the whole of human experience lay before her. The photo had been cut in half to get rid of the groom, leaving a tanned hand grasping Carla's bare white shoulder. There you go: even icy bitches like Carla can have a past where things were different. Other photos were of her at school, out on the lash with her pals as a teenager, ripping up her L-sign next to a red VW Polo.

I went to close the lid. Carla was becoming like a real person in my mind, and I didn't want that. She was the enemy right now, the one who'd snatched my kid, and the last thing I wanted was a twinge of sympathy for her. But another picture caught my eye and I paused, picked it up. It was the most recent one of Carla, by the looks of it, but still a few years old. She was sitting on Darren's knee.

Darren?

I was pinned to the spot for a moment, I don't mind saying. This did not compute. Darren was one proposition and Carla was another, and never the twain shall rub shoulders. Or so I thought. But like I said, only for a moment was I flummoxed. Everyone knows everyone in a town like this, and sooner or later they're going to shag them or fight them. Mind you, I had Darren down for fighting her.

Under the photo was a diamond engagement ring. I looked at it, rubbing the 22ct gold between my fingers, thinking back to when me and Jane had got engaged. But only for about five seconds. I was here for evidence, remember?

One last scout around the grottier corners of the flat and I found it. I stared at it for ages, hardly breathing at all. Everything around me was silent. Nothing existed except me and this evil little fact.

It knocks the wind out of you, reality does.

7.

There is a song by Michael Jackson called 'She's Out of My Life', and it means a lot to me. Around the time me and Jane split, it was all I heard in my head. You'd think that would turn you nuts but this song didn't. It's a special song, and fitted my situation like Michael Jackson's glove fitted his hand. But it wasn't about Jane. I didn't give much of a shit that she was out of my life after the initial trauma. It was about Kelly, my little girl. It's about every quiet moment that could have been filled with her.

And they *were* filled with her, those lonely moments. You close your eyes and swear you can smell her hair. You see her soft, light brown face, clear blue eyes. Sapphires in the desert, Jane called her when she was a baby: the perfect mix of white and black, cold and warm, her and me. We looked down at her as she slept, all new and sated on mother's milk, and wondered how she would turn out. I still do.

Then I open my eyes.

Sounds odd, what I'm about to say, but until me and Jane split I hadn't really thought of myself as having a daughter. I knew Kelly was mine, of course, but I didn't feel the connection. When she was born, I didn't feel no different. I didn't go around acting like a dad, and that's because I wasn't one inside.

I'm painting myself as a bit of a bastard here, but I'm not. The difference between me and a bastard is that I can look back and see it, point at that period of my life and say I was no good. Right up until the point when I discovered that leaving Jane meant leaving Kelly as well, in the end.

It cuts like a knife.

That's what the injunction was about. Jane stopped letting me see my own daughter, so I'd had to go round and throw gravel at the window like a lovesick teen. And that's what I was, in a way (although I was in my twenties by then). Any good father would be lovesick if they weren't allowed to see their kid. Like I say, cuts like a knife. Which is probably why I ended up crashing that house party with a machete.

It wasn't for Jane or Kelly. Don't be stupid. It was for him, that cunt of a boyfriend Jane was knocking around with. And I wasn't going to use it. Of course I wasn't.

I mean, come on.

What do you think I'm capable of?

I just wanted to scare him, let him know that there was already a family here — broken though it may be — and that he was walking on thin ice. Fuck up once and you're under. And by fuck up I mean try and replace me as her dad. Or try and turn Kelly against me. Or anything, really. There was a long list of potential fuck-ups he could make, and I'd be there waiting for him if he ticked a box.

So the machete was mostly to help him.

Keep him on his toes.

But I needn't have worried too much. Kelly was a good girl. She knew what she was about and where she came from. Love between a child and her father does not recognise injunctions, curfews nor threats. She stayed in my life, and it had stopped cutting like a knife.

Only it was starting again now.

I didn't know where she was.

But I knew one thing. If someone had hurt her, touched her or upset her in any way, I'd show them what cutting like a knife feels like.

Starting with Carla.

8.

They must have known I was coming.

I could tell as soon as I stepped inside the Alma. Every punter in there carried on drinking and ignored me. One or two looked up but didn't bat an eyelid. And that smelt wrong to me. When I walk in a pub around here, people bat eyelids. Especially in a pub like The Alma. Someone must have tipped them off. They'd all had a chat about it and decided to play it calm, act like nothing's up. And if you don't believe me, hear what the barman said when I went up and ordered a Famous Grouse and a bag of salt and vinegar crisps from him:

"I see you're back."

See? So I'm not paranoid. I can judge situations and read between lines.

I looked over my shoulder, craning my neck to get a view down there. "Well," I said, "it's good that you can see my back. 'Cos I can't, for the life of me."

I can play it calm too. I can play it loose and easy and sardonic, no problem. You have to. No point being all keyed-up and frothing at the mouth. There's too much at stake.

He ignored my comment and got on with serving me a Famous Grouse. I was looking around the room, sizing up the threats of violence, locating any alternative exits. Things could kick off in here. I couldn't see Carla, though, which surprised me. I was sure I'd heard her say about this dump being her local, a quiet little enclave where no one judges you, so long as you're the right colour.

"You can have this one on the house," the bloke was saying, pushing me a double, "but then I want you gone. We don't want none of your antics here. Right?"

See what I mean?

"Antics," I said. You'll note the absence of a question mark there. I was interested in the word and wanted to voice it myself, feel the shape of it in my black mouth. "So, what, you've got me down for swinging from the light fittings, have you? Reckon I'm gonna pull a knife and rob someone?"

"You know full well what antics I mean. And if I see any of them I'll have no hesitation in calling the coppers."

"Whatever you say, boss," I said, wincing at the whisky. "I'm just here looking for someone. I'll be out of your hair when I find her." I glanced at his bald head. "Out of your scalp, anyway."

"She's not here."

"Who ain't?"

"The one you want."

"How do you know who I want?"

"Because there's no other reason for you to —"

"Frank."

That's not me saying that last one. It was behind me, a female. And you can guess the one. If you think it's a tad unlikely that my daughter's kidnapper would just step up to me like that, imagine how I felt. I was all set for a blade in the kidneys. Carla could be like that sometimes.

Frank wasn't a happy barman. "Bloody marvellous," he was grumbling. "I thought we agreed you'd stay back there in the —"

"It's my problem. I'll deal."

"But he's just gonna carry on —"

"No he won't. Let me do this."

"But... at least let me call the —"

"Frank!"

I hadn't actually seen her yet. I wasn't sure what I'd do when I did. She was stood right behind me, three or four feet away. She'd stolen my daughter. She knew where Kelly was. She was working for Graven. I could snap her neck. Or at least break her jaw. I turned.

She wasn't there.

"She's gone and sat down, mate," said the barman, nodding at a corner table. "Any funny stuff and I'll have no hesitation, got me?"

I told him I'd be good so long as he gave me the crisps, which he'd forgotten as yet. He tossed me a bag, scowling. They weren't the flavour I'd asked for but I let it go. Sometimes a compromise is in order.

And I don't mind cheese and onion.

Carla's hands were clasped and resting on her legs, which were clamped together very tight. Her mouth was the same way, pursed so hard you could see the muscles popping out in her bony cheeks. Her back was bolt upright and she was facing away from me slightly. You don't need a degree in body language to work out how nervous she was. That's because I'd put her on the spot. I'd come right into her lair and demanded cooperation. And she was doing alright so far. I put a photograph of Kelly on the table.

The evidence I'd found at her digs.

"You got some fucking explaining to do," I said.

"Where'd you...?" she started saying, picking it up. "You've been in my flat, haven't you?" Her voice was wavering. Seemed like she was more upset than nervous. She'd thought long and hard about what she'd done and realised it was wrong. Fair play to her. But it didn't help me.

It didn't help Kelly.

"Never mind that — where is she?"

She looked at me straight for the first time. There was something funny in that look. Hatred?

"Alright," she said. "I'll tell you. But I want you to promise something first. I want you to swear that you'll never, ever come looking for me again. And I want you to put your hand on this photograph when you swear it."

She placed the snap on the table. It was from when Kelly was about five. She was on a little bike in the back garden of my old house. Just before it was taken she'd fallen off and cut herself, and you could see the plaster. I'd put it on myself, lining it up perfectly with the creases on her knee.

"Go on, put your hand on it. Swear on her life that you'll stay away from me. Swear it!"

People were watching me. Frank up at the bar. A couple of lads over there, both of them munching pork scratchings. An old lady in the other corner, stretching out half a Guinness. All eyes on me. I could feel them.

I put my hand on the picture. I had to close my eyes. I saw Kelly there, crying about her knee and asking for a plaster with a crocodile on it. We didn't have any of that sort left, so she had to have a tiger. I opened my eyes again.

Don't get weak now.

It made me want to puke, swearing on Kelly's image for a treacherous cunt like Carla. But I did it. I said the words she wanted to hear, then slipped the photo in my pocket, adding: "Where the fuck is she? *Now*."

Carla blinked. I think some of my spit had gone in her face. She didn't like that and I thought she was going to send it right back, but she just wiped it off. The jewel in her ring glinted blue at me.

"She's gone because of you," she said, nice and slow, still looking like spitting but not. "You need to face that, Leon. It doesn't matter how people try and help you, in the end you're gonna have to —"

"The fuck is this?" I said, getting up.

Frank grabbed something behind the bar and held it where I couldn't see it. "I'll have no hes-itation!" he shouted.

After a very long hesitation I sat down. "I asked *where* she is, not how come she's there."

"She's..." She stopped and took a deep and

shivery breath. "If you want to know where she is, maybe you should go back where you did it. Go there and try to work things out for yourself."

"What? Are you on about the VIP? Are... do you mean Destiny?"

"I've said all I'm saying."

"She's at Destiny? What the fuck's she there for? Is someone looking after her?"

"You swore on your daughter, Leon. You stay away from me now — I've told you what you want to hear. Now go, please."

"I ain't going nowhere. You ain't told me *shit* yet. All you told me is fuckin' *riddles*!"

"Frank?"

"Don't look at Frank! Look at me, you fuckin' slag! You stole my fuckin' daughter and I want her back! Now!"

Frank raised a baseball bat over his head, shouting: "You take your hands off her!"

"I'll take your fuckin' *head* off *you*, you come at me with that thing!"

"Frank! He's hurting me!"

Old Frank was some sort of white knight at heart. He came sliding over the bar, knocking empties everywhere and slipping on a wet bar towel when his feet touched down. He righted himself and took a swing at me. He was a left hander, like Babe Ruth. But where Babe Ruth was very good at swinging a bat, Frank was shit at it. I ducked.

The bat cut through the space where my head had been and followed through, hitting Carla in the shoulder and decking her. I laughed and planted my fist in Frank's fat belly. I could feel the beer sloshing around my knuckles, like I was leaning into a balloon full of warm tea. I laid another one in, hoping to burst that balloon. If you're gonna do it, mean it.

There was actually three pork scratching lads, not two. The other was coming back from the bogs just then, doing himself up. The other two slid off their stools and faced me, arms wide. No scratchings now, just three pairs of clenched fists and a couple of smirks at the prospect of kicking my black arse.

Fine.

Only one of them approached in the Queensbury manner, the other two skirting round the back like dirty pack hounds. I made a note of their unsportsmanlike behaviour and feinted a right at the one to the fore, following through with a left uppercut that waved adios to the end of his tongue, which happened to be between his teeth at that moment. Nice teeth, they were. Especially the ones at the front. I nutted him, waving adios to them as well. Someone hit me on the back of the head.

I hadn't forgotten about the other two, just wasn't set up to receive them in the manner they deserved until now. I grabbed one by the throat and held him like that while I whipped my left leg out at a right angle, winding the other and possibly breaking a couple of ribs. I don't know karate, honest I don't. Alright, I did take one or two lessons as a kid. But this kind of stuff comes natural to you if you just relax and let the mood swing you. I've got to admit, though, it helps to have a hard head. Especially when someone launches a stool at it.

I took it on the left ear, squishing the lobe and leaving it a tangle of flesh and gold. Shame, because I'd bought that ring new this morning. Hurt quite a bit as well. But do you know something? I quite liked it. It suited the mood I was in, putting a nice, bitter taste in my mouth and flooding my veins with turmoil. I smiled at the person who'd done that to me. It was Carla.

Everything went quiet for a moment as I looked at her. I'm not sure but I think it might have been in my head, the quiet. Maybe it was in her head too. Neither of us was speaking but it seemed like we were saying thousands of words to each other, just with our eyes. No, not thousands, just a few. But big ones. Important ones. I just didn't know what they were.

"Still do that, do you?" she said.

"What?"

"That."

She nodded at the table where we'd been sat. In the ash tray was a cheese and onion crisp wrapper, balled up tight in a pyramid shape. I stared at it, confused.

That's when Babe Ruth knocked me out.

9.

LEVEL 2: VOCAL ALERT

1. *Make judgement on whether vocal alert is genuine distress call or part of sexual congress. NB: client may well have requested and paid for vocal alert as an optional extra (eg: screaming, moaning, begging)*
2. *Upon arrival at scene, if alert is found to be non-genuine, apologise to client in a discreet manner and leave*
3. *If alert is genuine, deal with it*

Security is all about preparation. Getting your environment right, setting up the correct procedures, having the appropriate tools at hand for every eventuality. On top of that you need well-trained personnel, good men and women who know the drill and do not fluctuate from it. In the case of Destiny Gentlemen's Club, obviously the good men and women were just men, and only one of them. Plenty of women there, of course, but they were not designated security professionals. And they weren't good.

I grabbed the appropriate tool (locking up the security cabinet after me) and headed for the stairs.

I'd designed our alert scale myself, basing it on ones in prisons and other institutions around the country, but adapting it for the particular demands of the sex industry. I'd started off with eighteen levels but boiled it down to four. Barely was my hand on the banister when the second one kicked in.

10.

"I love this song."

You can smell a Beamer.

In a good way.

'Baby I want you come...'

Something going on in the engine produces a fragrance that is not unpleasant. But not quite pleasant, either. Those Germans knew all about that. Frankfurters — no one's going to class them as fine dining. But no one's going to turn one down, either. Especially not in a bun, a squiggle of mustard and red sauce on top.

It's like that with the Beamer smell.

"It's Robbie Williams singing it, you know."

"You think I'm thick, do you, Dux?"

"No, I was just saying it's —"

"You think I didn't know that Robbie Williams was in Take That, don't you?"

"I was just —"

"Don't underestimate me, Dux. Last person

who underestimated me, you know what I did
to 'em?"

"What?"

"I destroyed 'em."

"Yeah?"

"Yep."

"Who was that, then?"

It was all washing over me, the Beamer smell
and the voice droning on about destroying
Robbie Williams. I was neither asleep nor
awake and my head hurt. Hurt pretty bad, actually. I didn't know where I was, either. Actually
I did: I was nowhere. Not Earth, Heaven nor
Hell. I was in that place high up, where the stal-
lion meets the sun. But in a Beamer.

"Are you doubting me, Dux?"

"Eh?"

"Are you calling me a liar?"

"When did I say that?"

"Are you saying this person I destroyed don't
actually exist, knowing full well I ain't at liberty
to name him for fear of incriminating my ass?"

"No! Look, all I meant was —"

"Why would it incriminate your ass, Sid?"

"Shut up, Gnash. I'm having a word with
Dux, here."

"I was just wondering. Just thought maybe
you destroyed 'em with your ass, or summat."

"How would I do that? *How* would I fuckin'

destroy someone with my *ass*?"

I closed my eyes and tried to get back to where I'd emerged from, block out all that external bollocks. But the Beamer smell kept coming to my nostrils, nagging at me. *Think*, it was saying. *Think about me*. So I did.

And remembered that the Beamer smell is an interior one. Which meant... I dunno, something.

It means you're inside a Beamer right now, you twat. A black Beamer, to be precise. The one that Graven's boys were following you in.

It was right, the Beamer smell was. I wanted to thank it but it disappeared before I could, replaced by an altogether more rank affair.

"Fuckin'... who did that?" the main voice was whining. "Who shit in my Beamer?"

"That was me, Sid."

"You fuckin'... Don't you *ever* drop one like that in my Beamer again, Gnash! You do and I'll destroy your... I'll fuckin' *kill* you!"

"I was just showing how you can destroy someone with your ass. You got a fart bad enough, you could probably kill someone."

"Shut the fuck up."

"Sid, I think —"

"You can shut it as well, Dux."

"No, I'm serious, you ought to —"

"I'm serious as well! I've had enough of

your —"

"Sid! It's *him*. The spade, he's come round!"

I had things straight in my head now. I was in a car with three of Graven's twats. One of them had something terrible inside his guts and another had a fragile ego. The third was the one from in the abbey earlier on. I knew this because my eye popped up a fraction at the word "spade". He was sitting next to me on the back seat, pointing what looked like an Uzi machine gun at me. The car stopped. Hard.

I rolled into the foot bay.

"Sid, he's fallen into the —"

"Don't you ever... EVER call a black person that again!"

"What's the fuckin' problem, Sid? I'm only calling a spade a —"

"Gimme that."

"What?"

"The Uzi. Giz here!"

"W-why?"

"Do you trust me, Dux?"

"Y-yeah, but —"

"Come on, give. That's it... Good, now... You think I'm gonna shoot you?"

"Well, no, but I don't like you pointing —"

"You think I won't shoot you 'cos I'm your mate, eh?"

"Yeah, but it's dangerous to —"

"What if I told you I was half-black?"

"But you ain't."

"How'd you know?"

"You ain't half-black, Sid!"

"Shut up, Gnash!"

"But how can you be half-black? You got ginger hair!"

"I *told* you — It ain't ginger! It's fire blonde."

"Whatever, you ain't half-black."

"Oh yeah? And what about Ryan Giggs?"

Seemed like the right moment to do something. That rank smell had worked like a dose of smelling salts, shaking my senses up and getting my head working through the pain. The data was flowing in: who was where, how big and strong they were, where the gun was, who had bollocks, who didn't, who was racist, who wasn't. I reached up for a handful of headrest, intending to pull myself up and knock out all three in one fluid motion. But my arm didn't reach that far. It didn't reach anywhere at all, being stuck.

The Dux one flinched away from me, going: "Sid! He's... he's...!"

"Ah," said Sid, pointing the Uzi at me now. "We got a wide-awake one here. How's your head, bro?"

I closed my eyes for a think. No way was he gonna pull the trigger on me. I had him down for no bollocks and I can spot that sort a mile off. I could feel what the problem was now: handcuffs. Cold and heavy and not a chance of wriggling out of them with my big hands. But no matter.

Seriously, this was no bad turn of events. I had no clue how I'd gone from the Alma to here, but it was all to the good. I was being taken to Graven.

To Kelly.

"Miserable fucker," Sid was saying to me. "I'll get you answering me in a minute. You just wait."

He drove on for another few minutes. It was dark outside. Dux and Gnash were peering down at me, their obscured heads bobbing with the contours of the road. And it was quite a bumpy road. Like a farm track.

"Here'll do."

The car stopped and the three neds got out. I was invited to join them, and I did. No point in kicking up a fuss here. A fuss could be kicked up when the time came. And by then I'd have talked my way out of these cuffs.

It was no farm track. The road was asphalt but fallen into disrepair. There were buildings all around, all of them industrial and derelict. This was the old Billings Estate, on the edge of Makin. Some of the girls had plied their trade up here before coming to Destiny. You could see why. A girl and a punter could get up to anything inside those rusted hulks of former factories and warehouses, and respectable society need never know.

I'm no fool.

I know that an Uzi and a derelict estate don't add up to a bright future.

11.

Don't panic.

You can deal with neds.

"What's you got?" said Sid, the leader. He was ten or so yards off, his homies flanking him like bodyguards, Uzi trained at my knees.

"Nothing," I said. Truthfully. "But you know that, right? You frisked me already, right?"

They looked at each other, hissing quiet blame.

"Look, you might as well get on with it. No one's here to stop you. Gimme what I got coming, eh."

"Hold your horses, nigger," said Sid.

"What did you call me?"

"Yeah, but... I mean, I thought it was OK to —"

"You wanna say that word to me again, white boy?"

"I don't mean it like that! I'm saying it in the

good way. You know, the way you're allowed to say it. Like NWA — niggers with, erm..."

I turned and started walking towards the nearest building — an old metal castings plant, I think.

"Oi! Where's you — ?"

"You wanna do it inside," I said. "Out here in the open, you never know who's watching."

I carried on in there, smirking a bit. I couldn't believe what twats these were. If that's the level Graven was operating at, I'd been overestimating him. He still had my Kelly, though. As long as he did, I'd tread careful.

They followed, bickering.

I marched on, walking faster all the while. If they didn't keep up, I was going to walk on through the building and out the other side. Probably find some kind of rusted old machine edge around here to break these cuffs. Then they'd have some explaining to do when they got back to Graven.

"Mate!" one of them shouted. "We... we ain't gonna kill you. We just wanted to shit you up, like. 'Cos of you roughing up Dux, in the abbey."

"You're not gonna shoot me?"

"I don't think so, no. It's Dux — he can't fight his own battles."

"Oi!" shouted Dux. "That ain't true!"

"Yes it is! You said he was a massive cage

fighter!"

"I... I just said..."

"And you never told me he was a brother! I ain't pluggin' no br —"

Sid stopped there because I was coming right at him, slowing up not a bit as I bore down on his ass, as he would put it. A change of tactics, this was, in light of how useless these lads were turning out to be. Why break off my cuffs when I could get them to do it with a bit of intimidation? He jumped out of the way but I kept after him, surging on at a steady pace.

"Oi!" he was whining, "I'm your mate! It's me who saved your life here!"

"Take these fuckin' cuffs off, then."

"Alright! Just stand still, OK? Right, that's good. Dux — get his cuffs off."

He chucked some keys at Dux and pointed the gun at me.

"We shouldn't let him go," said Dux. "He'll turn on us."

"I'll plug him if he does."

"You said you don't plug brothers."

"Just undo him!"

Dux went behind me. Took him over a minute to get the key in the hole, he was shaking so bad. I stared at a dot on the wall the whole while, thinking about Kelly and imagining the dot was her, far away but I could just about see her. Then the dot started moving, and eventually flew off, looking for other cockroaches or whatever it was.

Soon as the cuffs were off I went after Sid. He aimed at me but didn't have the balls to fire. I'd judged him correct there. When I finally cornered him he dropped the gun and put his hands up, crying.

"Please, I swear I never meant to —!"

"Where is she?"

"What? Please let me go and I'll —"

"Where's Kelly."

"I dunno no Kelly!"

"Tell me where she is and I'll let you live. Don't, I'll gut you with a big knife. It's that simple."

I don't know why I'd said that about a knife. I didn't even have a pen-knife on me, let alone a big one. I picked up a bit of corroded iron and moved in.

"P-please! Don't kill me!"

His face was soaking wet with tears and snot. He put his arms over it but I yanked them down, scanning his head, looking for the softest spot to plant the sharp end. To me he was no longer a person, just a piece of work I had to do.

I could sense his two pals behind me, both a long way off and staying that way. Treacherous cunts, standing by and watching their pal get dispatched. I ought to do them instead of this one. He should ditch them and get some proper friends. Friends who watch your back, fight your corner and never let you down.

Friends like Darren.

12.

Darren.

Ah, where are you, Darren?

There had never been many times when I'd had to ask that question. He was just *there*, Darren was, making sure you're never alone when you don't have to be, giving you a strong arm when you needed it or a laugh when you wanted to share one. He had a funny laugh, actually, Darren did. Jane used to say it sounded like a seal, and if she closed her eyes she could picture him trying to clap his little flippers together. We had a chuckle at that. All of us, including Darren himself, flapping his flippers. That was Darren for you. He could have a laugh.

But he knew when to take things serious, too.

I can't even remember when we first met. If you live in one place your whole life, there's always going to be someone you can trace right back to the start. You went to school with him, play-school before that. Your mums used to get together for a yak, leaving you two toddlers to wrestle for dominance on the carpet. They brought you into this world within an hour of each other, in the same maternity ward.

Even when Darren went away at eighteen we stayed close. Things were quiet at first but I'd send him little parcels with food and mags and CDs, and he'd write letters. He's got into a fight in a bar in Belfast and broke someone's leg. He's got a girl up the spout in Bosnia but she thinks he's an American called Marlon. He's just done his first kill. I've still got that letter. Still got all his letters.

Somewhere.

He wanted me to come when he went to join up. Be a laugh, he'd said. Guns, action... seeing the world. We can leave this town behind us, sweep away all the trouble and bad feeling and get back to what's important: mates, loyalty, living life to the full and experiencing new shit every day. And I wanted to go, really I did. I knew he was right and that we were both perfect for the army. But he knew I was right as well. He must have. I was getting married. Jane was pregnant with Kelly. I was doing my HGV license. Darren had one life in front of him and I had another.

It was hard to face that at the time. Harder for him, I think. I could see his point of view. In a way, I think he was jealous. I mean, I'm not thick. I could see he still held a candle for Jane.

I couldn't worry about that. She was with me now. You ditch a girl, you lose your rights over her.

But you don't let that stuff get in the way of friendship, do you?

13.

"I can get you stuff."

Plausible deniability.

That's what they do with the US president. Don't tell him about all the bad stuff so he doesn't have to lie about it when reporters come sniffing. Any bad shit goes down with a US government stamp on it, the Prez stays clean and fragrant. That's what you had here, going the opposite way down the chain of command.

"I can get you herb, solid, skunk. You want a brick? I can get you one. I got smilies, bennies, mitsubishis, glass —"

"You swear on your mum's life you never heard of Graven?"

"I do swear it, mate. This Graven shit is a new one on me. Does it bring you up or down? Sounds like a downer. Hey, you want skag? I can get you —"

"Graven is a person," I said, looking out the

window. The world was pitch black. "A cunt."

"Shit, he sounds like one. And he's got this Kelly, you say?"

"*I'm* asking the questions, you're answering them. Right? And driving. Keep your eyes on the fuckin' road."

"No probs, mate. I'm just glad to, you know..."

"Be alive, I realise that."

I was in the front this time. The other two lads were in the back, cuffed together. I'd threaded the cuffs through the armrest to keep them still. I didn't trust them. Anyone who can sit by and watch his pal potentially get killed with a rusty iron bar is a wrong 'un in my book. But they had time to learn. These lads couldn't have been more than two years older than Kelly. Could be they even knew her. They'd better not, though.

I had higher hopes for her than that.

"I ask you summat, mate?" Sid was saying, coming off a roundabout into the dual carriageway. "Who are you?"

"Thought I told you *I* was asking the questions?"

"I know but, you know, you ain't asking none."

He smirked at me. He wasn't so bad, this one. Bit confused about his racial heritage, though. I told him a bit about myself. I had nothing to hide.

"Brothel bouncer?" he said, speeding up a bit to overtake a truck. "You serious? That sounds like a fuckin' smart job, that. You hear that, Gnash? Hey, do you get to shag all the toms?"

"It's about protection, not exploitation," I said. "They get enough of that in their jobs."

"I heard about one of them, recently," Gnash was saying. "Brothel bouncer? Where'd I hear about a brothel bouncer?"

"I'm the only one in town, pal," I said. "And I'm on sabbatical, you could say."

"Hmm... You know, I think I might remember where I —"

"Enough fuckin' questions, right?"

I turned around. It was so dark you couldn't see their faces on the back seat, just the shape of their bodies, chained at the wrist like they were holding hands. "You two cunts heard of Graven or what?"

Two heads shaking fast.

Plus mine, but weary and slow.

"Don't you know nothing about what goes on around here?" I was saying. "Don't you wanna know who runs things? Who's sitting on top of the pile?"

Their shoulders shrugging.

My fists clenching.

"It's Booker," Dux was saying. I'd made sure

it was his right hand in the cuffs. He was the little one but you had to watch him closest. "Booker runs everything around here. Got guns and everything."

"Yeah, and he's a cunt!" shouted Sid, almost swerving off the road.

"Fuckin' hell, Sid! Don't say shit like that!"

"Why? He can't hear me, can he? And he *is* a fuckin' cunt! Give it a year and he'll be out of here. No, he'll be in the fuckin' *ground*, that's where he'll be. I'll fuckin' put him there meself!"

"My my," I said. "Such ambition.... I'm impressed."

"He don't mean it," said Dux. "He's just fucked off 'cos Booker stole his bird."

"I fuckin' *do* mean it! Yeah, alright, I am fucked off about Fiona. But that ain't it. Booker's just a piece of shit with a couple of hard mates. Take them two away and he's *fuck* all! You *gotta* see that, lads."

I was still shaking my head. The ignorance of youth. If they only knew that this Booker was just another link in the chain of command, another rung on the ladder that had Graven at one end and these twats at the other. Mind you, I was worried now. Working at Destiny, I'd never come across firepower. I had no idea it was so rife. And if ground troops like this Booker had it, I needed it too. I turned to Sid.

"You know you said you can get me stuff?"

14.

A BB gun.

A plastic fucking BB gun.

And there was me, calling it an Uzi.

I'll just pause for a minute while you have a good laugh.

Finished?

I got the neds to drop me off by the abbey, not far from where this whole affair got moving. I thought about going in there and checking out that stained glass again, have a closer peer at the burning man and see if I could find a few distinguishing marks that made him not at all like me, actually. Maybe, if I could do that, I could slow my heart down. Maybe I could shake that hunch that I was going to pay the ultimate price for my actions. But that's not true, is it? The ultimate price is Kelly. My firstborn.

My only born.

So, yeah, I had a BB gun. Which is basically

an air gun, but with... Well, it's an air gun. A nice one though. They'd come a long way since my rabbit-hunting youth. Which was just as well, because I was hunting more than rabbits now.

But I still didn't know where to start. What was it Carla had said? That seemed weeks ago now, although it was only a couple of hours. The lads said they'd picked me up in a playground behind the Alma, slumped over a swing with a Tesco bag pulled over my head, the plastic going in and out as I snored. What the fuck had those cunts at the Alma hit me with? Enough to obliterate a chunk of memory. I couldn't remember the last time I'd been sparked out. They must have used a sledgehammer, swung with ruthless eff...

Ruthless. Babe Ruth.

A baseball bat.

Maybe you should go back where you did it.

Go there and try to work things out for yourself.

Amazing how the mind works.

Remember one bit and the whole dam bursts.

I walked, BB gun inside my coat, eyes staring four slabs ahead. I went in the Onestop for fags and a can of something with a lot of caffeine. I needed food as well, in theory. But something told me not to bother. Press on. Do not dawdle.

I did just that, drinking and smoking and burping. A bus slowed, heading for my destination. I ran a few steps but let it go. I needed fresh air and clarity of mind. I needed to think, plan, get my head straight.

Destiny?

What was Kelly doing at Destiny?

She knew about the place. I wasn't one of those dads who could lie to their kid. She knew I did something to earn a crust, and she knew my skills and qualifications weren't in chartered accountancy. I look after escorts, I'd told her, an escort being a lady who entertains a gentleman. That was enough. I left her to fill in the blanks in her own time.

What? You think I was wrong to?

Look at it this way: was it better coming from me or from one of the vicious little cunts she endured school alongside? Believe me, some of them knew. Their dads were regulars, and shameless about it. So she needed to know, if only to soften the impact when the cunts started on her. But I hadn't told her where it was. She didn't need to know it. And that's not plausible deniability.

That's holding it back for her own safety.

I was at the end of the street now, looking down at row upon row of terraced houses. You couldn't tell one apart from the others. Some had families in, some old couples, some bed-sits. One was a knocking shop with my daughter in it. She had to be. Why would Carla lie about it? My phone started ringing.

"Kelly?" I barked into it. Like a twat.

Go on, have another laugh.

"Leon, thank goodness you've answered," said a voice that wasn't Kelly's. "Don't hang up."

"Who the fuck is this?"

"Leon, please, you need to tell me where you are. I will personally come and pick you up and there need be no fuss. I found your notes, Leon. I know that this is another scenario."

I wanted to hang up but I couldn't. I was having one of my moments, like I sometimes did and always at the worst time. Reality all around me seemed like it was slipping away, showing the nightmare beneath. If only I could snap out of it. If only I could get the phone away from my ear.

'But it can't work," he was saying. "The scenario is flawed, Leon, just like the others were. Synthesis is the only way to —"

A dog barked. I didn't know where — could have been a mile away for all I knew. All I cared was that it snapped me out of it enough for me to hang up and switch of the phone.

What a time for a wrong number.

15.

It takes the breath right out of you.

For a moment, as she opened the door of Destiny Gentlemen's Club, I thought it was her. She was the same age... same height, hair, beanpole figure and heart-shaped face.

But the eyes were brown.

And the skin, when you recovered, you saw it wasn't that dark at all. Cream without the coffee.

"Hello?"

But still you stared. Still you hoped and yearned and rationalised. It was the light. The moon was shining in through that coloured glass above the door, distorting her colouring. Yeah, that was it.

But it wasn't, was it?

"Er, wait there a sec."

She turned and walked off down the hall, showing a swing in the hip that put her two years older than I'd first thought.

"Dad! There's a bloke at the door!"

It was the same hall where the security cabinet was meant to be, but now there was just a coat stand and a shoe rack with a school bag chucked on it. She went into the waiting room, where you sometimes had fights on a busy night. Down the end, in the kitchen, you could hear an oven door being slammed. No one ever used that cooker. I'd flagged it up as a health and safety risk, but had anyone taken any notice? Had they hell.

What...

What the fuck? This was Destiny. *Destiny*, a fucking *brothel*.

"I help you, mate?" The bloke was saying it as he came striding down the hall, almost lunging for the front door and closing it a bit, jamming his toe behind it. Brown Eyes was going to get a bollocking later about leaving the door open on a stranger. A stranger with an Uzi-shaped bulge in his coat and a look of desperation about him, I realised, seeing my reflection in the door glass. "You lost, are you?"

"Lost?" I said, staring into his eyes.

"Do I know you?"

"Know me? You? No... no you don't. That's just it, ennit? You don't know me and I don't know who the fuckin' hell you are!"

The mum appeared at the kitchen door, oven-gloved and holding a backing tray. "You alright, Trev?"

"Trev's alright! It's me. It's Leon here who's fucked, ennit? Leon's being played for a right cunt here!"

"Oi, if you're gonna talk like that you can —"

"Where's my Kelly?"

"Oh God, it is you, isn't it? When I saw the paper, I wondered if you might try to —"

"Don't fuck me around! Just tell me the score. I've fallen for it, OK? You fuckin' win. Graven wins! He wants me insane? I'm insane. I'm a fuckin' nutter! OK? Now tell us the deal. Tell us what I do now!"

I think I'd made a breakthrough here. Whatever script he was sticking to, I'd knocked him right off the page. They thought I'd lose it and start smashing the place up but I was cutting to the chase, conceding the point without a fight. *Now* we could get somewhere.

"Erm, OK. Let me just... Wait here, OK?"

"Don't keep me waiting."

"I won't! I'll just, erm..." He pushed the door to and kept on pushing it, ever so gentle, hoping I wouldn't notice he'd shut it. Where had they found him? I've got to say, I was far short of impressed by Graven's people. You'd think he could have made an effort for me. But he didn't need to, did he? He was stringing me along just fine with bargain-basement chumps.

Mind you, must have been a job converting Destiny into this place so fast.

I looked through the door glass. There was net on the other side and you couldn't see much. The mum and dad were in the kitchen. Looked like they were talking at first but Dad turned his head and I could see he was on the phone, waving his spare hand around. Mum was looking at him, chewing her nails. She looked in my direction and let out a shriek that even I heard. I didn't like that. Made me feel like a stalker. Or an escaped lunatic.

"You got three minutes!" I shouted through the letterbox. "Three minutes and I'm coming in. Right?"

"Er, no, don't... I'm just talking to Gra... Gravesend."

"*Graven*, you twat! Where the fuck did he find you?"

"Yeah, sorry. Er, you'd better give me some privacy, OK? You know what Graven's like."

"Just *hurry up*."

I left him to it and went to peer through the bay window into the waiting room. The light was off in there and it was hard to see, street-light streaming down behind me. You could make out where the curtains were separated but I couldn't seem to look beyond it. Some big thing was in the way, made of material and some sort of frizzy stuff at the top, and — I jumped back.

I was staring right at her, the one who wasn't Kelly. Except...

Except it was different now. I couldn't see the skin or the eyes, only the shape of her. And I swear it looked just like...

Was it?

I mean, maybe it was?

Hadn't Carla said she'd be here?

"Kelly?"

I was quiet at first, gentle. Don't want to frighten her. She'll be scared enough already.

"Kelly, lift the window. Go on."

She just stared back at me.

"I'm here to save you, Kel. Come on!"

I turned and scanned at ground level. Plenty of gravel but nothing big. Then my eyes adjusted and I saw it, weighting down the base of a wooden bird table. I picked it up.

"Move back, Kel."

But she wouldn't. She just stood there like a shop dummy, staring back at me. Maybe they'd drugged her. Yeah, that'd be it.

"Alright, stay right there!"

I half expected her to move now, but she didn't. I went to the far panel and lobbed the brick through the window. There was loads of jagged glass so I got the bird table and knocked it all away. Then I climbed in.

She was screaming. The poor girl was...

Light comes on, Mum and Dad stood there, horrified.

"Kel," I'm saying. It sounds like a word, not a name. Sounds like the noise an animal makes, a bird of prey, thwarted at the last moment as he swoops for his quarry. It's not Kelly.

Sirens behind me, two or more of them coming from different directions, some way off but getting near. Suddenly they stop, almost in unison.

Hands around my waist, hauling me out. I twist around and aim a backhander to the face, knocking Darren on his arse.

Darren.

16.

1. *The alarm is a piercing tone that hammers against your skull and shakes your very soul*
2. *Do not panic*
3. *Do not lose control*
4. *Locate source of alarm*
5. *Eradicate*

I do find that cricket bats are a better all-round security implement. Your common baseball bat, being heavily weighted to one end, operates solely on the concept of centrifugal force. It's for swinging, in short, which means you need enough swinging space for it. Meanwhile your cricket bat is weighted quite evenly all over. You can swing it just the same, but you can also poke, drive, sweep, cut, pull and defend with it.

I used a MRF Wizard, like Brian Lara.

Sometimes I took it out back and messed around with a ping-pong ball, imagining I was Lara on his way to 400 in Antigua. But right now I was creeping along the landing with it, holding it out front, edging towards the source of that Level 2 vocal alert. I stopped to wipe my eyes.

You need 20/20 vision in this game.

The vocal alert had taken the form of screaming at first, but now it was dying down into a series of sobs and moans. She was in trouble and I had to act fast. But what was he doing to her? If he was strangling her she wouldn't be able to make sounds like that. If he was beating her, you'd hear it. He must have been using a knife, cutting her so bad that the life was draining from her. I braced myself for blood. A lot of blood.

I wiped my eyes again. My whole face was wet. I didn't know why.

A door opened behind me. Room Three, which was meant to be empty. I turned.

It was dark but I could see the girl's outline.

"Mummy?" she said, rubbing her eyes. A shaft of moonlight was coming from somewhere, lighting up her little face. Her teddy was slung over one shoulder, like a fireman saving a small child from a burning house. "Mummy, I can't sleep. Too noisy."

She opened her eyes. Sapphires in the desert. Just like I remembered them.

She turned them on the bat I was still holding.

"What you got, Uncle Darren?"

"I'm..." I had to keep wiping my eyes. "It's Daddy, love. Your Daddy's home."

"Daddy away," she said. "Mummy say Daddy on lorry trip."

"I was, Kelly, but I've come back."

The vocal alerts had stopped, but there was another kind of alert going on now.

Level Three.

I went over to her and stroked her hair, took her hand. She'd grown. She was up to my belt now. "You gotta go to sleep now," I was saying, tucking her in.

I could barely see through the tears as I left her room. But I had to see. I had work to do, incidents to deal with. A punter had gone rogue and one of the girls was in trouble, possibly her life in danger. It was the new girl. She wasn't new, really. Just that I hadn't ever been able to understand her properly, make a connection with her. But she was still mine.

I kicked the door in. There were no locks but I wanted to make a statement, put the shits up anyone who had ideas. You have to get the upper hand in these situations. Getting your job done is paramount and failure to do so cannot be countenanced. I entered the room, bat held high.

They were both out of bed, she in her gown, he with his jockeys on, bent down to pull up his trousers. You can't hesitate. Take your best chance when it comes.

I swung the bat hard. It connected just above the left eyebrow and sent him down.

17.

Darren the lifesaver.

Darren, my true friend.

Do you see why I'd been ringing him now?

He got me by the hand and dragged me through a hedge into the driveway of the next house, then up the side path and into the back garden. All the while his nose was pouring blood, courtesy of my backhander. It splashed down his chin and onto his nice blue V-neck, and I felt awful about it. I had every intention of paying for the dry cleaning, or even getting him a replacement, and I wanted to tell him that. But he wouldn't let me.

He put his hand over my mouth and went: "Shhhhhhh." Just like that, all drawn out and slow and quiet, staring into my eyes in the darkness. I was nodding, understanding what he meant. This was Darren and he knew the score on most things. In a second or two I heard little noises out front — the odd footstep, scraping, a burst of radio.

Darren tapped my forehead and I blinked. He pointed at the back fence, which looked about five foot high. We crept down the lawn, finding a gate, but it was padlocked. Darren ignored it anyway, vaulting the fence in one elegant move, making no more sound than one flap of a dove's wing. Darren used to be a Royal Marine.

I didn't, but I got over the fence somehow.

From there on it was easy. Two connected alleys, a quiet crescent and we were on the canal path, walking casual and heading for some teenagers lurking under the bridge up ahead. Any sane person — even someone useful like me — would think carefully before pressing ahead with that route on a normal night. But not Darren.

With Darren, it's the teenagers who think carefully about what they're doing under that bridge, and do they really need to be there just now. They don't, it seems, and they slope off out the other side and up the bank.

"Darren?" I said quietly, testing the waters. He didn't shush me this time. "Darren, I been trying to get hold of you for —"

"I know."

"Oh, right. You got my messages, then?"

"No. I got a different number now, Lee.

Changed it a couple of years back."

Lee. I liked that. It was like a totally different name, a secret identity that I only got to use when Darren was around. I'd missed it.

"Oh. Well, how'd you find me?"

"Just knew you'd be here."

"How?"

He shook his head, which I thought was a strange gesture. We were passing under the bridge now. It smelled of fresh spray paint and fags. Someone had done a giant comedy cock on the damp bricks, white paint still dripping.

"Is it to do with being a Marine?" I said. "That how you found me?"

"Everyone's looking for you, Lee. Ain't you seen the papers?"

"What papers?"

"No, I suppose you'd avoid them, wouldn't you? Too much reality."

"What are you on about, Daz?"

We were out from under the bridge now. Across the canal was a retail park. Behind us a bank of grass led up to the park. Darren stopped and kicked a stone into the water.

"You can't go doing stuff like this, Lee."

"Stuff? What stuff?"

"You know what." He seemed to remember something and turned to me, looking into my face. "Alright, maybe you don't know. I can't even begin to understand all this shit that's going on with you. People have tried to explain it to me. I even spoke to..."

"Who?"

He got some fags out and didn't offer me one.

"Who'd you speak to, Daz? Was it Graven? Did you speak to Graven?"

He snapped his gaze to a spot behind me, like he'd heard something up there. Always the soldier. The moonlight came from under clouds and lit up the scar tissue above his left eyebrow. It was pink and shiny. I think he'd taken a bomb blast in Bosnia or something. He didn't like to talk about it.

"Look, Daz," I said, "it's alright. Really. There are some things I just gotta do on my tod. You... well, you got enough of your own problems, things you've seen in combat and that."

He was looking at me again. He still hadn't lit the fag in his mouth. "I heard they gave you a kicking over at the Alma," he said. "I don't blame them, you know. You should leave Jane alone, bothering her like that in her local. And she knows you were snooping around in her flat. She don't hate you no more, Leon. It's called moving on. I've done it as well, and now it's your turn."

I was feeling dizzy, like some drug was kicking in.

"I can help you, Lee. I'll come see you, in

the —"

"Daz!" I said, shaking off the dizziness. "Don't you see? I gotta find Kelly! I gotta find her now!"

He shook his head, kicking another stone into the water. "Go to Birchwood."

"Birchwood? What?"

"You wanna deal with your shit, go there."

"What the fuck is this? Some kind of fuckin' Halloween game? Halloween was last week, Daz. I need to find Graven! I need to find Kelly!"

"But you wanna play games, though, don't you? Come on, let's fucking play. She's at Birchwood. She's... Graven put her there."

I just stared at him for a bit, bouncing from one eye to the other. "And Graven? What about Graven?"

"Can't help you there, Lee. Only you can sort that one. But do yourself a favour, eh? Do everyone a favour: when you find him, get it sorted. Once and for all, like. Maybe..."

"Maybe what?"

"Maybe you should finish him off."

"Eh?"

"I meant... ah, nothing."

Calming down now. Trying to slow my heartbeat, get on top of things. This was serious shit and I needed answers. I grabbed his jumper and posed a question:

"How come you know all this?"

I knew he'd switched off from me now, said all he had to say. He was waiting for me to finish. Waiting to go home.

I had the BB gun in my pocket. I wasn't sure why I remembered it at that moment but I did. I wanted to get it out and fire it in Darren's face, punish him for... I swear I don't know what.

"Oi!"

It came from behind me, a female voice, quite young and carrying a lot of bolsh. For some reason I thought it was Kelly, and I turned. I couldn't breathe. Some teenagers were up on the bank, hands in pockets, hoods up.

"Oi!" it came again.

You'd never have known from their outlines that one of them was female. How could I ever have thought a voice as harsh as that could be Kelly's? It was more like her mum's.

"Are you hearing me or what?" she said. "I want me money."

"Money?"

"Half now, half later, you said."

"What for?"

"Are you thick or summat? For ringing that number and saying all that "where's Kerry?" shit to some bloke called Leon. So cough up, you fuckin' mong!"

I got the BB Gun out and fired it at them, making them disappear. A minute or two later, after I'd chucked the gun in the canal, I remembered Darren in time to catch a glimpse of his back disappearing into the tunnel. I shouted his name as I went after him, but I knew I'd never catch him.

18.

I couldn't make sense of it. Birchwood? What was someone like Graven doing at Birchwood, let alone holding a girl there? There wasn't even a building, unless he had keys to the very public one in the middle. And this is Graven we're on about here.

We're talking *influence*.

I was carrying on down the canal path, thinking this. I didn't know where Darren had gone. Didn't care.

Did care.

And there's no point denying that. But friends end up betraying you, always. Even best ones. Especially best ones. I couldn't worry about that. I had to think and breathe and walk. Towards Birchwood.

I was there in ten minutes. Or maybe two hours. My throat was parched but I ignored it, thirst wouldn't hold me back. I walked along

Birchwood Road, skirting the perimeter wall, looking through the trees. Could it be true? Or was Darren just feeding me bullshit? Why not? Carla had fed it me, saying Kelly was at Destiny. No one was at Destiny.

Not even *Destiny* was at Destiny.

Which meant Destiny had to be somewhere else.

"Yo, nigger!"

Sometimes you react before thinking. Quite often I did that, actually, but sometimes it's like a taut wire snapping, a catapult fired. Before my next breath I had the kid in a headlock, face-down on the wet pavement. That's how keyed up I was.

"Oh cm om!" he was trying to say, chewing concrete. I took my knee off his head. "Oh come on! I ain't having this shit! They call each other niggers in films all the fuckin' time! Ain't you even seen *Pulp Fiction*?"

"You call someone nigger, you are a nigger," I said, still sitting on him. His pal Gnash was a few yards off, stepping around like he needed a piss bad.

"Yeah, and I told you — I got a bit of black blood! My great-granddad was a sailor from Liverpool and he was black like coal! I swear! That makes me a nigger, bro. And *that* means I can say it to other niggers."

"Well, I ain't a nigger, so you can shut your fuckin' white mouth!"

"But..."

But bollocks. I was off down the road. There was less trees round the other side of and maybe I could get a better view. Of what? I still couldn't see how Kelly could be here. Or if she was, she was well hidden. No way was I gonna find her without some more intelligence. There was no way around it:

I needed to find Graven.

"Mate!" the lad was shouting, running to catch up. He was heading for a kicking, this Sid character. Another time I'd give it freely. "Mate, just hold up a minute! I got summat for you."

"I got summat for you as well: free fuckin' dental job, via my black fist."

"Look, I understand why you're being like that." He was alongside me now, waving his arms around. His pal had more sense, being about ten paces behind. "It's natural for black people to have a chip on their... Alright! Alright. I won't say no more about the righteous struggle. I just wanted to let you know, well..."

He looked left and right. Birchwood Road was deserted. When he turned his head I saw the five inch long slash, butterflied up on his cheek.

"Where'd you get that?" I said. Not that I gave a shit. "Cut yourself shaving? Give it a couple "more goes and you'll get the hang of it."

"I don't mind it. I've adjusted to it already, see? Only got it stitched half an hour ago and I'm easy with it. That's what I'm about. I adapt and react — that's how I'm gonna take over here. People will call me Scarface from now on."

"People will call you cunt-face. Same as they do now."

"Whatever. I ain't fuckin' around here. You put in an order, I've come through for you."

"What order?"

"You know what."

"A gun? You already gave me a gun. A shit one."

"This ain't about the gun. I'm on about the other thing you wanted."

"What, fuck sake?"

He chewed his gum five times. "Graven."

My balls tightened.

19.

I was driving.

I insisted.

Even with all this shit going on, I still found it in me to enjoy the smooth handling of the Beamer. Even a knackered old 316i like this one. Kraut engineering stays the course, no matter how hard you thrash it.

I was thrashing it now.

"Just tell me," I said. It was the second out of three times I was going to say it in a polite and patient manner. Three strikes and you're out was being very generous, I thought. Next time, he was going to find out how it feels to be out.

I made sure he wasn't strapped in, then looked across his lap at the passenger door handle. Seemed like an easy movement.

Reach. Open. Shove.

You're out.

"Just through the grapevine, you know," he

said, touching his stitches. "Like Marvin Gaye."

"How did I know you'd mention Marvin Gaye?" I said.

He gave me an innocent smile. "Do you think black minds think alike?"

"What I think is that I'm gonna ask you one more time. How do you know Graven is at this address?"

The lights I was heading for turned red. Fuck it — no one was about. I bombed them, swerving easy around the cyclist coming over the junction just then. I looked in the rear-view and watched him wave a fist at me. Such misplaced rage. I slipped my eyes sideways and checked Gnash on the back seat. Maybe he'd give me some aggro when I dumped his cohort on the tarmac. I worked out a follow-through move to tag on the end of that without even taking my right hand off the wheel. Should be easy.

And it looked like it was gonna happen. I said: "Five."

"What?"

"Four."

"What? Four what?"

"Tell him, Sid!"

"Three."

"Get off me, Gnash! Tell him what?"

"Tell him how you know Boo... erm, Graven is where he is!"

"Two."

"Tell him!"

"One."

"Alright! Alright, I'll fuckin' tell you, if it means so much."

"Tell him, Sid!"

"Fuck off, Gnash! You touch the back of my head again and I'll fuckin' *stripe* you!"

"Come on, just tell the bloke."

"Alright, well... What I did, see, is I thought about what you said. Chain of command, you said. In any kind of organisation, you're only dealing with the one above you. And that's Booker. You try to get past him to the one higher up, you're making Booker sort of like unemployed, know what I mean?"

"Redundant."

"Yeah, that. You're making him redundant, like my dad is. So he's gotta protect his ass. He's gotta make the one above him *invisible*, so you don't even try to get to him."

"That's very clever," I said. "You got initiative, son. I can see you climbing a ladder one day. Cleaning windows, perhaps."

"You asked, I'm telling, right? I did some asking around, sticking my nose where it weren't wanted, and I turfed up the name Graven. From there, it was a piece of piss. The higher ranks, they don't move in the same circles like us ones. You gotta go to different places to find 'em, different pubs."

"Graven don't drink in pubs."

"Course he don't. But his boys do. And..."

"And his boys won't talk. He's a secret, pal. To plebs like you he don't exist."

"Ah, but... do you know what I've found, mate? There's always a weak link. No matter how loyal you think your homies are, there's always one who'll let you down. There's always one fuckin' *cunt* who —"

"You don't know that, Sid," the lad in the back said.

"Fuck off, Gnash! Dux grassed me and you fuckin' *knows* it!"

"But you don't —"

"Dux?" I said, getting confused here. "Isn't he your other mate, the skinny one?"

"Forget Dux," said Sid, touching his stitches again. "Dux is just a cunt. He's history now anyway, good as. I'm on about the one who betrayed Graven. Up in the Chequers. Big feller with a footy top on, tats all over on his —"

"What team?"

"Eh? Who cares what — ?"

"Come on, convince me. Spread some detail. Who's name was on the back?"

"Well, it was, erm... blue. Everton, I think. And it was that striker... what's his name?"

"Rooney?" I said.

"Rooney? Mate, you're a bit out of date there. Rooney got sold to Man Utd fucking years ago."

"What? Oh..."

"You feelin' alright?"

"Shut up. Go on... what about this bloke in the Chequers?"

"All I had to do was bung him some skunk. Got him talking and within ten minutes I got an address."

"So that's all you got? An unconfirmed address? Fuck sake..."

"No, mate," he said, "it ain't about the whether or not Graven's there. It's about what he showed me. It's about what he offered me in exchange for a block of skunk."

"Sid."

"Shut up, Gnash, I know what I'm doing. I gotta tell him."

"Tell me what?"

Sid just looked at me, licking his lips. Looking for the words.

"*What?*"

"He... the bloke showed me pics on his phone. Of a bird. A young bird, too young."

"What? Who? What did she look like?"

"Well, you couldn't really see but, you know, she wasn't white."

"You dunno for sure."

"Shut the fuck up, Gnash! I'm helpin' the man. You think I'm enjoying this? The man needs to know!"

"But..." I didn't know what to say, what to ask. My fingers kept squeezing the wheel and letting go. I gripped again, hard, not letting go. Deep breathing, firm chin. Common sense. Perspective. "You dunno it's her," I said. "Could be any black girl."

"You'd best pull in a minute, mate."

"Bollocks."

"Just for a sec. Trust me."

I didn't even notice doing it. One minute I'm going sixty in a thirty zone. Next I'm tucked in between an Astra and a Mondeo.

"I got this for you," said Sid, opening his jacket. Street light wasn't coming in from this angle but no mistaking what he had in there. Yellow light off the dash hit the dark metal and made it shine a bit, like sweat oozing out of a sick person.

No way was this one a BB gun.

"It's fuckin' heavy. You takin' it or what?"

"How much you want for it?"

"It's a gift."

"A gift? Fuck off."

"I swear. This is an offering, from brother to brother."

I sighed. "That all you wanted me to pull in

for?"

"No, that's cos of what I'm gonna tell you next. This feller in the, erm... Liverpool top, he said the girl's name was Kelly."

20.

You bring them up with such hopes, dreams of what they'll be when they grow up. Prime ministers, athletes, scientists... whatever. None of that matters, really. All you want is for them to grow up safe.

And for nothing bad to happen to them.

"It's just in this next road."

I was following Gnash. Sid had stayed with the car because he didn't want to bring it too close, he'd said. Gnash was showing me the way to Graven's new place.

The new Destiny.

"I been thinkin'," he said, spying round a corner before stepping out. "I remember where I seen a brothel bouncer recently. Remember I said I seen one? Yeah, it was a thing on telly."

Destiny. After all your hopes and dreams and wishes, this is where they end up. Cross out scientist, put down prostitute. Slag. Whore.

"Feller cuts up a hooker and the bouncer beats him up bad, then has to go on the run from the local crime boss."

Only it wasn't her, was it? She hadn't *chosen* this path. She'd had it thrust on her.

"I think it was Denzel Washington."

I'd had it thrust on *me*.

"Playing the bouncer, not the crime boss. The crime boss was Joe Pesci, I'm sure of it. You know him? He's fuckin' class in *Goodfellas*. Hey, d'you like pizza?"

Kelly. Sapphires in the desert. Blue crystals, glinting in the sand. You're paying for my sins. *You're* paying because *I* fucked up. He's making you pay.

Graven.

"No? I could fuckin' *murder* one meself. Anchovies, I likes. Fuckin' hate pineapples on a pizza, though. What's all that about?"

Graven.

"Anyway, look, it's in there. Number 33 — the blue door there. See it?"

I'm walking.

Lights on upstairs but none down. That's because the windows are boarded up. Front door's out of commission too — no way I'm getting in there. I slip round the side. Got to be an entry somewhere. How do the punters come and go? But there's nothing in the back yard.

Windows boarded up here too and the back door's made of breezeblock.

A sound behind me.

I slip behind a shed and peek out.

Just some twat, a kid like Sid and Gnash. There's chipboard where the kitchen window should be and he knocks on it, waits, stepping trainer to trainer. He turns — I swear he's seen me. But he couldn't have.

Anyone who saw me right then would have shit.

Seconds later the board lifts outwards from the bottom. There's hinges at the top — nicely done. The lad climbs in and it comes down.

I wait a few minutes. Thinking.

About Kelly.

Rubbing her eyes, sleepy.

Trying to save that teddy from a burning house.

I step up to the window and knock. Not too hard, not too soft. I'm looking at my watch: forty-seven, forty-eight, forty-nine... Chipboard goes up. Glazed eyes looking out at me. Another ned, too stoned to react and save himself.

I point the gun at him and blow his fucking head off.

All of him seems to disappear. There's a big area of red slop on the wall behind him and a bit of smoke, like he's exploded. I climb in.

There's a sink you have to clamber over but they've filled it with bricks to help people like me. I can hear voices now, upstairs. Shouting and screaming. Female screaming.

I hit the lino, finding where the stoned lad went. No time to check what state he's in — sidestep around the destruction and into the dining room. That's what we called that type of room in our old house, between the kitchen and the living room.

"Where's your Daddy?" Jane would say.

"Daddy 'mokin' in dinie room!"

I loved the way she used to say that. 'Mokin'.

"Kelly!" I'm at the foot of the stairs, booming that name. Front door's open and a nice breeze is coming in, bringing a whiff of distant bonfires. A noise in the front room and I stick my head round the door. There's a lad behind the couch, plain as the white sock on his ankle, which is sticking out the far side.

"Come out now and I might spare you," I say, calm.

He does it, hands up. It's Sid's other pal, the one from the abbey. Dux. I never really took to him. He's staring back at me, trying to smile. I don't think I return that smile. Whatever is on my face, he knows it's not good.

"Booker!" he yells. "Booker! Help!"

He's got one of them really irritating voices.

I put a bullet in his leg, aiming to both shut him up and give him a permanent limp for his treachery. His leg disintegrates at the knee. Funny kind of bullets in this gun. He looks at it, opens his mouth and passes out.

I'm looking at the gun as I back out toward the stairs. Doesn't say what it is but it's a big fucker alright. Someone's moving up there in the front bedroom. A whimper, female.

Kelly?

I run up, doing it in about two bounds. It's dark in the room and the light doesn't come on when I tell it to. There's a big double bed all messed up in the middle, stuff on it like bottles and little plastic bags. The floral patterned duvet is all bunched up on the far side, half fallen off.

It's breathing.

I go round there and wrench it off. It's a big duvet, and I have to keep yanking and yanking, like a magician pulling hankies out of his mouth. I get to the end and someone's hanging on for dear life. A girl, wet face and blood coming out of her nose. She looks up at me. The eyes do seem blue.

I crouch and look into her face. Could it be? Could she have changed so much? She seems to think so, the look of hope and eager-to-please on her face. But I don't.

No fucking way.

I lift the gun to shoot her. I want to punish her for not being my daughter. Someone jumps from behind the curtains and out the door. Male? Female? Clumping footsteps down the landing says it's a bloke.

I'm after him.

He's in the back bedroom now. Window's open and curtains billowing. I fire a shot on the off-chance, hitting the wardrobe. I reach the room and the air is full of talcum powder and bits of cotton. I stick my head out the window in time to see the last bit of him disappear over the back wall. Graven?

It *must* be him.

I aim the gun, hearing the running footsteps and waiting for him to appear somewhere. You can see all the little roads around here. Lights are coming on in upstairs windows all around, scared and angry voices in the night. Then I see him, a shape running through the allotments over there, knocking down beanpoles and disturbing new roots.

I'm out the window, hitting the grass and rolling over like you're meant to.

I'm over the wall and after him.

Sirens are getting nearer but we're heading away, towards Birchwood.

21.

LEVEL 4: OUT OF CONTROL

1. *Stabilise situation*
2. *Escalate problem to higher authority*
3. *When higher authority arrives, keep out of the way*
4. *Accept consequences*

I locked her in the en suite. She didn't like it but I had to do it, for her own safety. Rogue punter was incapacitated on the bedroom floor behind me still but liable to get up any minute, and I couldn't take chances. I had a job to do. There were procedures.

"Lee," he said, barely getting it out. "Lee, I'm..."

He was behind the bed from me but I watched him in the wardrobe mirror. He looked groggy as fuck but he was able to pull himself up a bit using the bedside table. I jumped on the bed and destroyed the cheap bit of MFI tat with two swings of my bat. He went down again, sprawling with his face in the plywood fragments and bits of glass from the framed picture I always kept on that bedside table. Straight away he lifted his face again, like a boxer who don't know when he's beat. Bits of glass and droplets of blood fell off his cheek onto the photograph. He craned to look at me, eyes trying to say what his tongue didn't know how.

"Lee, we just..."

I looked at the photo. A little family of three: one dark, one pale and the other a combination of the two. Whatever it had been, it was finished now. Everything was different now and I felt myself splitting apart.

Jane was banging on the en suite door, screaming for her daughter.

Screaming for forgiveness.

"Lee..." Darren was croaking. "Come on, think about this."

But that was just it, wasn't it?

I couldn't bear to.

I brought the bat down on his head again, finally stabilising the situation.

You don't have to think. Not when you've got procedures in place for all eventualities. I went downstairs and made a call, then closed my eyes for a few moments. When I opened them again, Graven was there. He was holding the lighter fluid from the security cabinet and a box of matches. He turned his eyes on me and said he'd take over now.

I wasn't sure about it. I really wasn't sure. But it was out of my hands.

I said I'll tell you why Kelly had been taken away from me and now I have done. Those are the details how I remember them and how I need them to be. Maybe there are other bits, I don't know. Memories fade over time, and although I could swear this happened only a moment ago it also seems like it happened a moment before that... and every moment going back years and years. And it will go on happening forever and ever until I stop it. But I *was* going to stop it. I was going to be with Kelly again.

This time I knew how to reach her.

22.

"It's diabolical."

"Isn't it just."

"He's done it before, you know. Eight times. No, nine."

"Three."

"What?"

"It says it in the article here."

"Where?"

"There, see? Bla bla... no less than three occasions since he was placed at the secure unit seven years ago, after being found not guilty due to diminished responsibility. The last time was two years ago, when he caused terror at a peaceful house party by threatening guests with a machete. Two years before that, he —"

"Yes, I can read. I still think it's diabolical."

"I know."

"His own daughter. Five, she was. Five years old."

"I know. It says it all here."

"I don't think people like him should be allowed to come back to the places they did their crime."

"He's not, that's why they're after him. Do you wanna buy this paper or...?"

I was in a corner shop just outside Birchwood Cemetery. I'd rather they ignored me, the old lady and the shopkeeper. I wanted them to carry on whatever they were gossiping about. But I knew that was asking a bit much, me out of breath, sweating buckets and covered in blood. The lady hobbled off out the door and the man tried to act like I was just another customer. He wasn't doing too bad, actually, although you could hear his controlled breathing.

I asked him for what I wanted. All of it behind the counter stuff. "I can't pay you," I said. "Sorry."

"Don't worry about it."

"I'll pay you tomorrow, right?"

"No you won't," I think he said as I was leaving the shop.

He was right, as it turned out, but I had every good intention at the time. When you look back, you can see that I, *Leon*, had nothing but good intentions at every stage along the way, and never intended to hurt no one.

It was quiet in the cemetery. No one was about except a couple of old dears, a middle-aged man in his Sunday best and someone on a sit-down mower. Still I felt quite tense, like this placid setting was about to kick off big time any second now. I looked again at the mower man. He was as old as the other three and about five foot tall, so I couldn't see him causing me trouble. Unless he had a Glock under them overalls. You never knew with Graven. You could never tell who he had influence over, who he had corrupted. But it wasn't the mower man who was getting me all keyed up. I didn't know what it was.

Maybe it was just excitement.

I was going to find Kelly.

If only I knew where to look. What if Graven didn't have her here, after all that? I'd chased him most of the way but lost sight of him at the end, and hadn't seen him come in here. But it felt like he was here somewhere.

I trusted that feeling. I had to.

I went to shout her name. If she was here I was going to find out. But I held my tongue on the K. Someone was staring at me, right over there by the big angel-type statue.

It was the Sunday best man.

"Leon," he was saying. Not shouting, but loud of voice. And firm, like someone getting respect from a dog. "Leon!"

I turned and went the other way, just wanting to get away from him. I know it doesn't reflect well on me but I couldn't abide his voice. I could sense things being derailed with that voice around, detailed plans getting fucked up just before they bore fruit. That's why I was running.

"Leon!"

I don't know what it was, but I found myself slowing. Not to a stop yet, but back to walking pace. I knew I'd get away from him at this speed but I also knew it wasn't going to work. All it was going to take was him calling my name in that way, just one more time.

"Leon!"

I stopped. There was a bench there and I sat on it, looking down at the big V formed by my legs. There was a lot of bird-shit on the path. The old man had reached me.

"You've caused me a great deal of trouble," he was saying, easing himself onto the bench next to me. Way too close for my tastes. I could smell the Fisherman's Friend he was sucking. "It's gone too far this time, Leon. You've caused a lot of people a lot of pain. Is that what you wanted?"

I could still run. Couldn't I? I could go and hide behind that big headstone there. I could run past it and keep running until I was back in the road, then...

Then...

"Leon!"

"Yeah! I mean no, I never meant no one no trouble. All I'm trying to do is get things sorted."

"I see. And what do you say to me?"

"Just... I dunno. Sorry, I suppose. I never meant it."

"Well, OK. But, you know, we could have talked about this. If I'd have known you wanted to try this again I could have helped you. It was always an option, but you never expressed an interest, Leon. You gave us to believe that all this was behind you. We've been exploring other channels, remember? Can you tell me some of those channels?"

I shrugged. I was watching a new figure, over the far side. Thought it was one of the old dears at first but no, this one was male. Couldn't tell much more though.

"Well, what about the buried letter? Remember that? You wrote down the thing you most wanted, the one thing that kept you awake at night and that you hoped to attain one day. Do you remember that, Leon?"

The male shape was getting closer. Seemed like he was looking right at me for a moment. It was hard to tell.

"You dug it up, didn't you? Before you escaped."

I shrugged.

"Can I have it?"

I got out the soil-stained letter. He opened it and read it, going: "Hmmm, I see." He folded it up again and gave it back to me.

But I didn't want it.

I didn't need it now.

"While we're at it," he said, "can I have my phone back?"

I gave him his phone, wiping it first because I think it had some blood on it.

"Thanks, erm... have you been hurt?"

"Cut myself shaving."

"Right, well... Leon, can you recall any of the other channels we've been exploring? Do you remember we talked about destiny?"

I flinched. Felt like someone had lobbed a stone at me. I turned, rubbing the back of my neck, but no one was there. Strange. When I looked back to the front again I could no longer see the male shape in the distance. I could feel myself panicking a bit, thinking I'd lost him. But then I saw him, over to the side. Much closer.

"Do you remember what your agreed destiny was? *Synthesis*, Leon. Do you recall what that means?"

It was Graven.

"Well, I'll remind you. It means reuniting disparate parts to make an organic whole. Now, we were trying to achieve that in therapy, weren't we? But we could use the opportunity we have here. What do you think about that?"

It was fucking Graven, plain as day and shameless, walking around in front of me like he owned the fucking place. Which, in a way, he did. Graven was the boss around here. Graven had influence.

"Of course, it's preferable in a controlled, safe environment, but not essential. This is your destiny, Leon. Go to Graven."

"What?"

"Go to him. Face him. Confront him. Accept him."

"Graven?"

"Of course. Who else?"

"What, you mean... You know Graven?"

The doc realised he was leaning in too close to me and sat back, trying to relax a bit. Any second now he'd cross his legs. All part of the show, trying to make it look like he was calm and in control.

He crossed his legs.

"I have met Graven, yes," he said.

"He's a cunt! Did you tell him he's a fucking cunt?"

"That is not for me to say, Leon. If you feel that way, you should tell him yourself."

"Did... Did you bring him here? Did you tell him to prance around over there like he owns the fucking place?"

"Graven is always here. This is where he lives. Remember?"

"But..."

"You need to make peace with him, Leon. Find a way to accept what he is and what he has done. Only then can you move on."

I looked at Graven. Didn't look like he'd seen me yet. He'd stopped strolling and was crouched down in front of a headstone, reading it. His back was turned to me.

I looked at the doc. He smiled and nodded. I think he might have spoken but I couldn't hear it any more. My head was full of sound, howling voices and clattering metal. I was confused and excited, elated even. It was like I'd been set up on one of those TV prank shows, but the host had revealed himself beforehand and wanted me to go ahead and walk on, knowing full well it was a trap.

Alright, I said. I'll do it.

Because I was one step ahead, wasn't I?

I went to Graven.

23.

The doc meant well, I knew that. I'd tried going along with his synthesis thing but it didn't work. I knew it could never work as soon as he'd said it involved coming to terms with things. Some things you can never come to terms with. Some things you just have to fight. To the death.

As I walked I could see figures in the trees, darting around a lot faster than people normally do in cemeteries. I was sure some of them were watching me, but I didn't care. I was up for it now. Graven was right there, only yards away. I'd found him. He was going to tell me where Kelly was. I was going to beat it out of him.

Only feet away now. I opened my mouth to shout his name but it didn't seem right. He'd gone beyond that. I'd kick him. I'd run right up and aim a boot up his arse. I started positioning myself to do that when he got up and stepped to one side, facing me.

He'd been waiting.

I knew it from his eyes.

All of this, everything was planned.

He waved one hand at the headstone, compelling me to read it.

I tried not to. Why the fuck should I do what that cunt tells me? But I couldn't fight it. He always got his own way. I looked at the headstone.

KELLY ROSE GRAVEN

BELOVED DAUGHTER OF
CARLA JANE GRAVEN

'SAPPHIRES IN THE DESERT"

"They left my name off," he said after a while. "I can't accept that. She was my daughter too, not just hers."

He looked at me.

"Fix it, will you?"

I stared at him, trying to burn holes in his brown skin, praying for that mole on his left cheekbone to burst open, all of his lifeblood pouring out and quenching this sacred ground. But I couldn't seem to make that happen.

I couldn't do anything.

"Put it on," he said again. "Write our name."

I got out the bag of stuff from the corner shop. I rummaged in it for the marker pen and knelt in front of the headstone, ready to write. I couldn't stop myself.

He was stronger than me.

"Synthesis, Leon!" the doc was shouting far behind me. I could barely hear him. At least two helicopters were hovering above me. "Synthesis!"

Still banging on about it, even now. He thought he knew the truth, that this brothel bouncer stuff was all a fantasy based on that film I'd seen on telly in the rec room, that I'd split myself into two: the knight and the dragon. Yeah, that was all true, but it was only half of it. The other half was that I knew it. I was fully aware of the game I was playing in my head. But there was no other way. This was the only way to slay my dragon. As long as I went through with it.

I dropped the pen and sprayed lighter fluid all over Graven.

The men were coming out of hiding now, running towards me. Some were holding walkie-talkies to their faces, others pointing guns at me. All of them were coppers.

The only thing left in the bag was a box of matches. I lit the whole lot and dropped it on Graven.

I crumpled alone onto Kelly's grave, paying for what I'd done like that man in the stained glass. The last thing I saw before the flames took me was the name I'd just added to the headstone, before the epitaph:

AND LEON GRAVEN

Crime Express is an imprint of Five
Leaves Publications

www.fiveleaves.co.uk

Other titles include

Trouble in Mind by *John Harvey**
The Mentalist by *Rod Duncan**
The Quarry by *Clare Littleford**
The Okinawa Dragon by *Nicola Monaghan**
Gun by *Ray Banks**
Killing Mum by *Allan Guthrie**
Not Safe by *Danuta Reah*
California by Ray Banks
Claws by *Stephen Booth*
Close to the Mark by *Allan Guthrie*
Speaking of Lust by *Lawrence Block*

* A6 format, with French flaps